# Harold's Fairy Tale

*Further Adventures with the Purple Crayon*

# Harold's Fairy Tale

*by*
*Crockett*
*Johnson*

SCHOLASTIC INC.

New York  Toronto  London  Auckland  Sydney
Mexico City  New Delhi  Hong Kong

ISBN        0-439-10469-6

12 11 10 9 8 7 6 5 4 3 2 1                    0 1 2 3 4 5/0

Printed in the U.S.A.                                             23

First Scholastic printing, February 2000

One evening Harold got out of bed, took his purple crayon and the moon along, and went for a walk in an enchanted garden.

Nothing grew in it. If he hadn't known it
was an enchanted garden, Harold scarcely
would have called it a garden at all.

To find out what the trouble was, Harold
decided to ask the king.

Kings live in large castles. Harold had to
make sure the castle was big enough to be
the king's.

He didn't want to waste time talking to
any princes or earls, or dukes.

This was a king's castle all right. It had tall towers and a big draw-gate to keep out people the king didn't want to see.

But when the draw-gate was drawn closed

it kept Harold out too.

Harold shouted for the king to come down
and let him in. But the gate didn't open.

He walked along the edge of the enchanted

garden beside the smooth wall of the castle

—until he thought of his purple crayon.

A person smaller than a very small mouse

would be able to get in.

Without even bending, he walked into a
very small mousehole.

He walked through the mousehole into
the castle. He invited the mouse in too,
but the mouse preferred to stay outside.

As he gazed around inside the big castle
Harold felt very tiny.

And a king might not pay much attention

to anybody who was smaller than a mouse.

So Harold used his purple crayon again.

He made sure he was as tall as four and
a half steps of stairs, his usual height.

Then he climbed up the stairs, looking
for the king.

He went up and up and up, until he got so tired he couldn't climb another step.

Luckily there were no more steps. He had reached the top.

He still couldn't find the king. But he

remembered kings sat on thrones.

The king's throne looked very comfortable.
Harold thought the king wouldn't mind if
he rested a few minutes.

He sat on the throne, wondering what it
was like to be a king and wear a crown.

He tried it, with the king's crown.

It was all right for a while. But the
crown began to feel heavy.

So Harold put it on the king's head.

As he thanked the king for the loan of
the crown, he noticed the king looked
sad—no doubt because of the garden.

He asked the king if the trouble was due
to a witch or a giant. The king couldn't
say which. He looked sad and helpless.

Evidently the giant or witch—if the king
couldn't tell which it was—was invisible.
But Harold told the king not to worry.

He set off to find the invisible witch or giant, brandishing his purple crayon. And —accidently—it made a hole in the wall.

The accident embarrassed Harold. But
the hole was the handiest way out of the
castle and he climbed through it.

When he looked down from the other side
of the hole, he realized he had forgotten
how high up he was.

He needed something tall to climb down
on, something as tall as a steeple.

To fill the hole in the castle, Harold put

a handsome and useful clock in it. He was

surprised to see how late it was.

He slid down the steeple, to find the
invisible witch or giant right away.

It wasn't a steeple. It was a pointed hat.

It was a GIANT WITCH.

The purple crayon made it plain—it was
an invisible giant witch. Well, no wonder
nothing grew in the enchanted garden.

How could anything grow, Harold said

to himself, with a giant witch tramping

around with big feet.

Now that he saw what the trouble was, all
Harold had to do was drive the witch out
of the enchanted garden.

Mosquitoes. Mosquitoes, Harold knew, will

drive anybody out of a garden.

The mosquitoes drove out the witch. They also were driving Harold out of the garden.

He had to make smoke to get rid of the mosquitoes.

And he had once heard somebody say that
where there's smoke there must be fire.

To put out the fire, he first thought of
fire engines. But he decided to make it
rain. Rain was easier.

The rain soaked everything—Harold too.

But, he said, it's good for the flowers.

He was right. Soon there were flowers.

Beautiful flowers popped up all over the enchanted garden, more than Harold was able to count, all in gorgeous bloom.

Harold thought how delighted and happy

the king would be when he looked out

from the castle in the morning.

And then, amazingly, the last flower
turned out to be not a flower at all—
but a lovely fairy.

She held out her magic wand as fairies
always do when they're giving somebody
wishes that will come true.

Harold couldn't think of a thing to wish
for. But, to be polite, he took one wish
and told the fairy he'd use it later.

Besides, Harold thought, as he started on his long walk home, a wish might come in handy sometime.

After all the excitement he suddenly felt
tired. And he stopped to rest awhile.

He sat on a small rug because the ground

was still somewhat damp from the rain.

And he wished—

He wished the rug was a flying carpet.

At once Harold felt it rise in the air.

It flew fast and high.

But when it went so fast it left the moon

behind, Harold realized he didn't know  how

to stop the carpet, or even slow it down.

He wished he'd taken two wishes from the
fairy, so he could wish the flying carpet
would land.

But he did have his purple crayon.

He landed the flying carpet in his living
room, right behind the high-backed chair
his mother sat in, knitting.

And he asked her to read him a story
before he went back to bed.